There is no one method
the ONLY way to learn to
learn in a variety of ways
an enjoyable and uncomplicated scheme
that will give your child reading confidence.
Through exciting stories about Kate, Tom
and Sam the dog, **Read with me**:

- *teaches the first 300 key words
  (75% of our everyday language)
  plus 500 additional words*

- *stimulates a child's language and
  imagination through humorous,
  full colour illustration*

- *introduces situations and events
  children can relate to*

- *encourages and develops
  conversation and observational skills*

- *support material includes Practice and
  Play Books, Flash Cards, Book and
  Cassette Packs*

Always praise and encourage
as you go along. Keep
your reading sessions
short and stop
immediately if
your child loses
interest.

Published by Ladybird Books Ltd
80 Strand London WC2R 0RL
A Penguin Company
7 9 10 8

Printed in Italy

Read with me
Kate and
the crocodile

by WILLIAM MURRAY
stories by JILL CORBY
illustrated by STUART TROTTER

Tom is at home.
He is in bed.

Sam has
a ball.

No, Sam, no.
You can't jump on the bed.

Tom has the ball now.

You can't have it, he says.

Come here, Kate and Tom,
says Mother.

Kate is not here, says Tom.
Kate is in bed.

Tom, tell Kate to come here,
Mother says.

Tell Kate to come here, now.

Come on, Kate and Tom,
says Mother.

Kate, this is for you, she says.
And Tom, this is yours.

Sam, come on and have
yours now, she says.
Come now, Sam.

Here is your hat, Tom,
says Mother.
And here is your hat, Kate.

Kate and Tom,
put your hats on now.

You must put this on
now, Kate.
And Tom, here is yours.

I must have this toy,
says Kate.

We must go to school now,
says Mother.

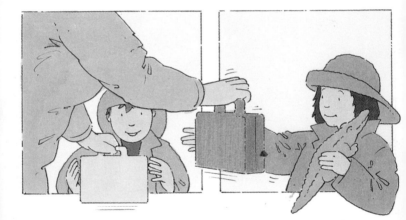

Here is your lunch box, Kate.
And Tom, here is your lunch box,
she says.

Come to the zoo.

Come on, Kate, we must
go to school now, says Tom.

Kate tells Tom to look.
Look at that, she says.

Come with me, says Mother.
We must go to school.
Come with me now, she says.

Here is the school.
In we go, they say.

Put your hat here,
Tom says to Kate.
And you must put
your lunch box on here.

The teacher comes up to
Tom and Kate.

Come with me, she says.
We must go in here.

Tom likes to read.
He looks at the boats.

I like to read, he tells Kate.
He tells the teacher
he likes to read.

Kate, says the teacher,
this is Suki.
Come with me, says Suki.

Come and play with me.
Kate likes to play with Suki.

Can you see this fish, Kate?
Suki says.
See that in the water.
It is like yours.

Look at this toy,
says the teacher.

It's for you to play with, Suki.
Now you can go and play.

They play with the toys.
I can put it in the water,
says Suki.

See that go in the water.
It can go round and round.

Come in now, please,
says the teacher.
Suki and Kate, please come
with your toys.

They all go into school.

Here you are, Kate and Suki.
You can have this.

Can you read it, Suki?
Yes, Suki says, I can read that.

Read that book to Kate,
please, says the teacher.
Yes, read it to me, please, Suki,
says Kate.

Suki reads the book to Kate.
The book says that
we must do it like this.

Can you see? says Suki.
We must put it here.

Here is your lunch box, Kate.
Come with me
to have your lunch.

We go up here.
We all go up here for lunch.

Stay with me, Kate, Suki says.
We stay here to have lunch.

We are all here now.

Do this with the sand,
says Suki.
You can do this with the sand.

There is some water over there,
Kate says.

The toys can stay in
the water and go round and
round, she says.

Now they can go up
over the sand.

Now we can do this, Suki says.
Please come and do this
with me, Kate.

This can go round here,
and that can go over there.

I can just put some sand on
here, and you can put that sand
over there, Kate says.

I can put that up for you now,
says the teacher.
Now we can see all of it.

It can stay up there
for all of you to see.

I can put Tom's rabbits
over here, she says.

We can see all of the rabbits
up there.

We can hop like rabbits,
round and round.

We can hop up here and
we can hop over there.

Rabbits hop like this and
they can hop like that.

I can hop,
just like you.

The teacher says, Just look at this, just look at all this sand.

Please put all of the sand in there.

The sand must go in
there now.
Wait there, Kate,
and Suki can do it.
She can put it all in there.

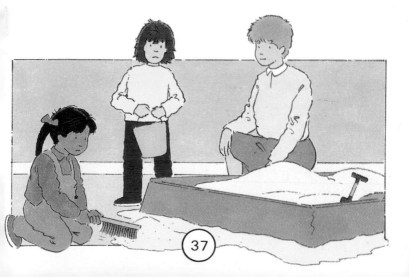

Come here all of you, please,
says the teacher.
I want to read this book to you.

Just come over here, please.
Just stay here with me and
I can read the book.

There are rabbits in this book.
And look at this…

You can all go home now,
says the teacher.
I have your lunch box,
Tom tells Kate.

And your hat is over there.
Wait for me, Kate.
Please wait for me, says Tom.

Look, there is Sam.
Now we can all go home.

Words introduced in this book

Number of words used..............................34

All Key Words are carried forward into the following book, Book 6 *The dream*.

They play with the toys
in the ....

water   fish   sand

Suki reads the
.... to Kate.

boats   book

rabbit

LADYBIRD
READING SCHEMES

Ladybird reading schemes are suitable for use
with any other method of learning to read.

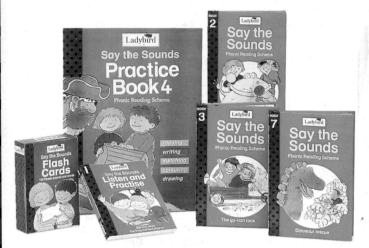

Say the Sounds

Ladybird's **Say the Sounds** graded reading scheme is a
phonics scheme. It teaches children the sounds of individual
letters and letter combinations, enabling them to tackle new
words by building them up as a blend of smaller units.

There are 8 titles in this scheme:

1 **Rocket to the jungle**   5 **Humpty Dumpty and the robots**
2 **Frog and the lollipops**   6 **Flying saucer**
3 **The go-cart race**   7 **Dinosaur rescue**
4 **Pirate's treasure**   8 **The accident**

Support material available: Practice Books, Double Cassette Pack,
Flash Cards